To Leslie, Thank you for being such a great friend I'll always be there for you no matter what the situation I love you!
Happy 21st Birthday
Love Jessica

For Michele

===

Copyright © 1994
Peter Pauper Press, Inc.
202 Mamaroneck Avenue
White Plains, NY 10601
All rights reserved
ISBN 0-88088-616-1
Printed in China
7 6 5 4 3 2

A Friend is Someone Who...

by Beth Mende Conny
Illustrated by Lyn Peal Rice

PETER PAUPER PRESS, INC.
WHITE PLAINS, NEW YORK

Introduction

Friendship is a sheltering tree.
—Samuel Taylor Coleridge

Our friends have been around almost as long as we have.

From the days of tricycles and dolls, through puberty and college, marriage and careers, our friends have been witnesses to our personal histories.

They've seen us shine and falter, laugh and cry, fall in and out of love. They've been there with words of advice, encouragement, with helping hands and loving hearts. They've given us their best and demanded that we be our best. And through it all, they've taught us the meaning of friendship, that deep bond that creates, in Aristotle's words, "a single soul dwelling in two bodies."

A Friend Is Someone Who... is a special collection for that special friend. It celebrates the many warm and wonderful ways friends enrich our lives, and acknowledges that our friends—be they ones we have known for years or just for weeks—truly are our significant others.

B.M.C.

A Friend is Someone Who...

Remembers your birthday
but forgets your age.

A Friend is Someone Who...

Shares your views about life, love,
and chocolate.

A Friend is Someone Who...

Accepts you on a bad hair day.

A Friend is Someone Who...

Has all the loyalty of a dog
but none of its bite.

A Friend is Someone Who...

Is critic, confessor, and cheerleader—
all wrapped in one.

A Friend is Someone Who...

Doesn't laugh at you in a leotard.

A Friend is Someone Who...

Agrees that sweets should be one of
the USDA's food groups.

A Friend is Someone Who...

Will swap clothes, kids, and romance novels.

A Friend is Someone Who...

Knows you never outgrow the gift of
a stuffed animal.

A Friend is Someone Who...

Will listen to you tell the same story
100 times but will fall asleep only twice.

A Friend is Someone Who...

Knows your husband (boyfriend) almost as well as you do.

A Friend is Someone Who...

Understands your edible complex.

A Friend is Someone Who...

Gives you what your kids cannot—
sympathy when you're sick.

A Friend is Someone Who...

Keeps your innermost secrets safe—
even the one about you and Fabio on a
deserted tropical island.

A Friend is Someone Who...

You can be a kid with.

A Friend is Someone Who...

Like a mirror, helps you see
who you really are.

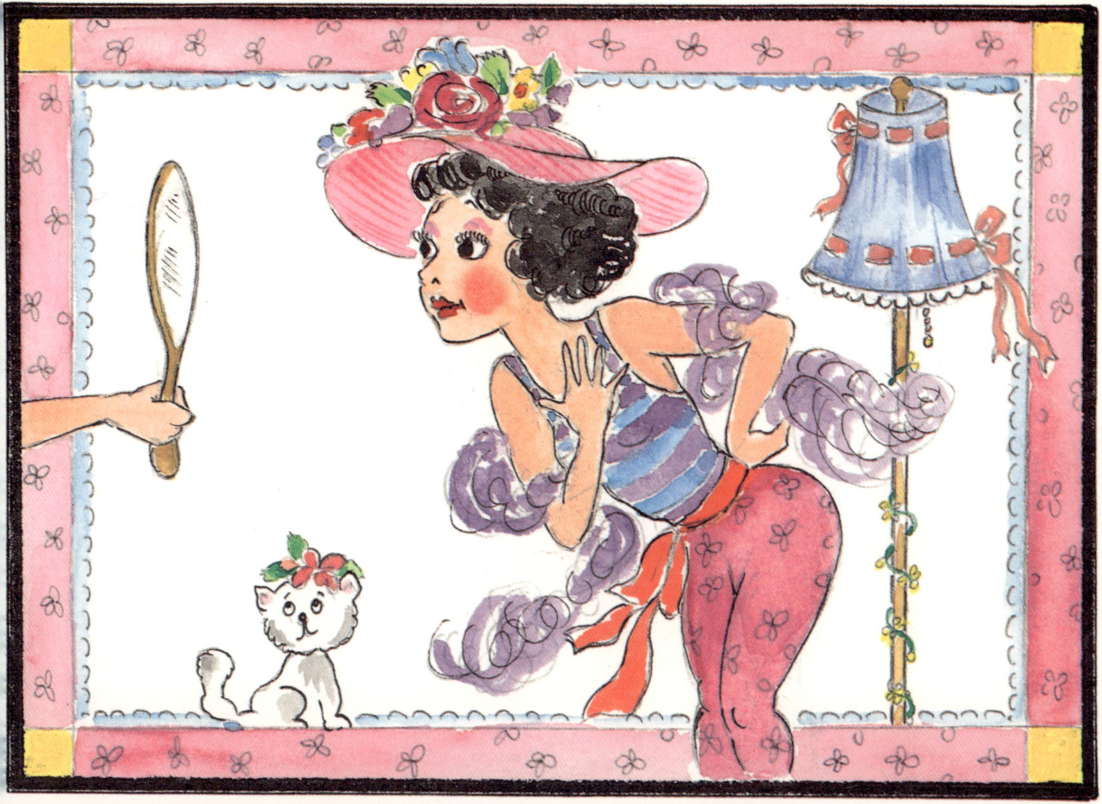

A Friend is Someone Who...

Never tires of marathon telephone sessions.

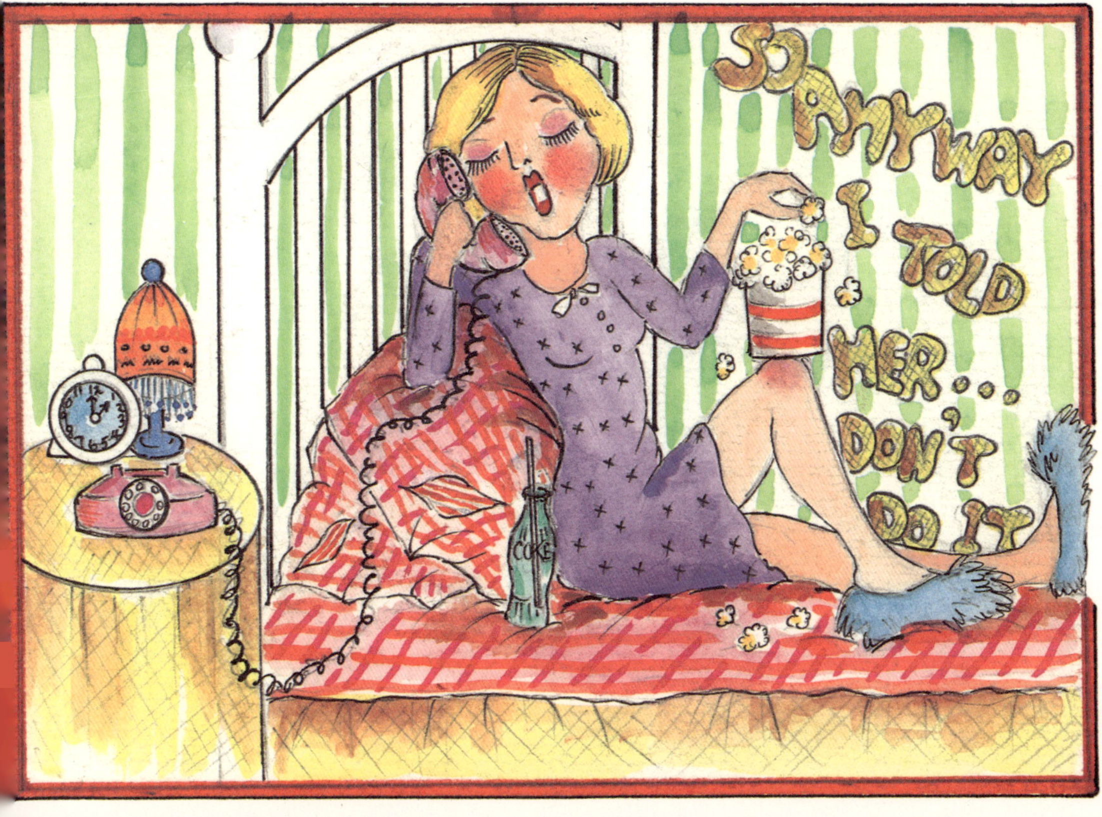
SO ANYWAY I TOLD HER... DON'T DO IT
COKE

A Friend is Someone Who...

You can run away with—to the movies.

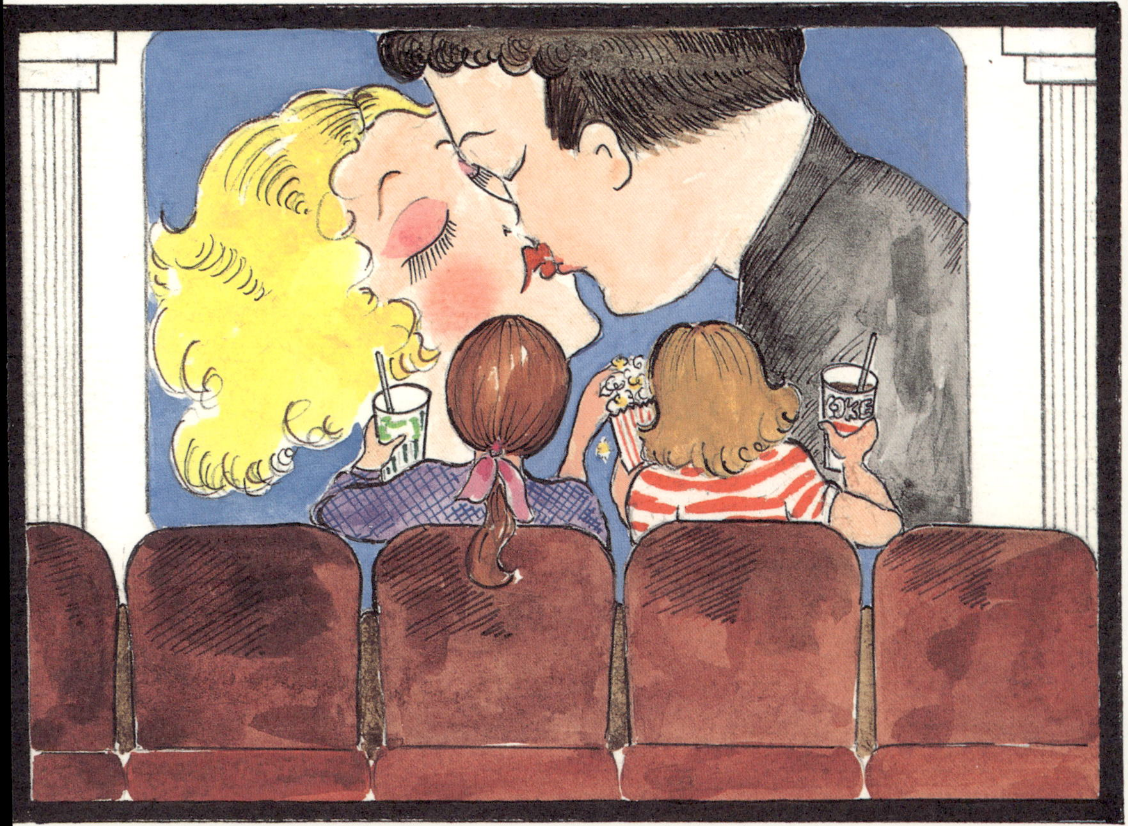

A Friend is Someone Who...

Has a sixth sense for a sale.

SNIFF
SNIFF
SNIFF
BIG SALE
FELINE'S BASEMENT
BARGAIN BONEANZA

A Friend is Someone Who...

Expects your best but accepts your worst.

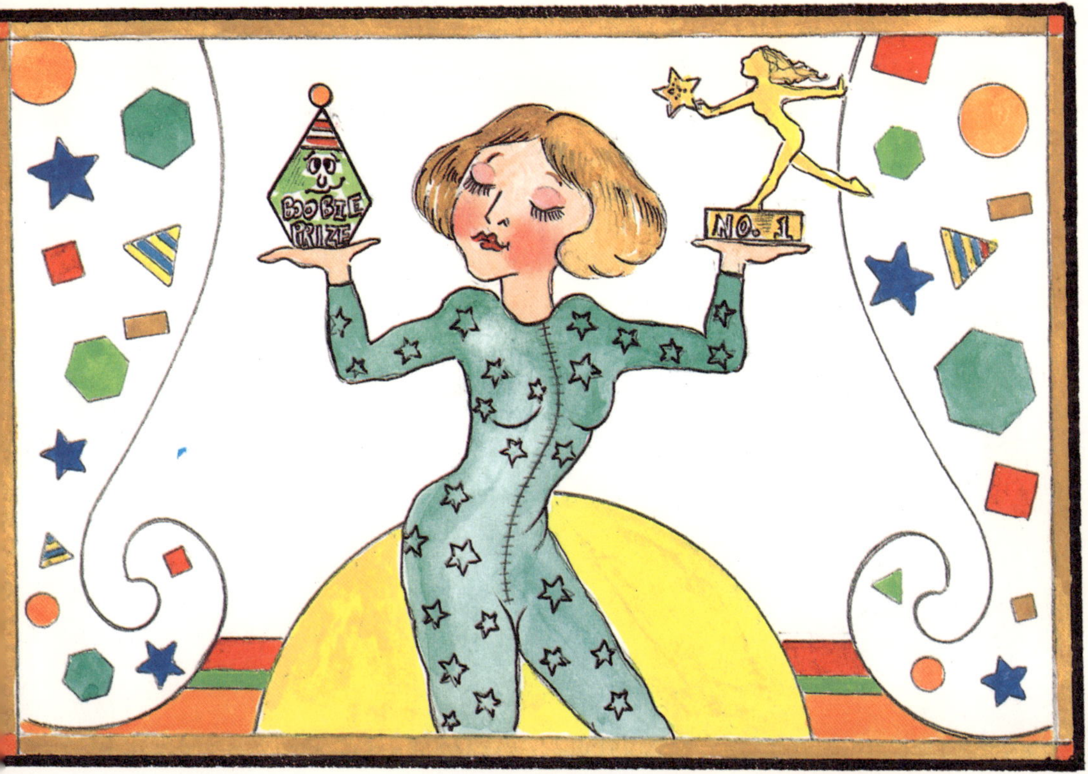
BOOBIE PRIZE
NO. 1

A Friend is Someone Who...

Sees you through thick and thin—
and not so thin.

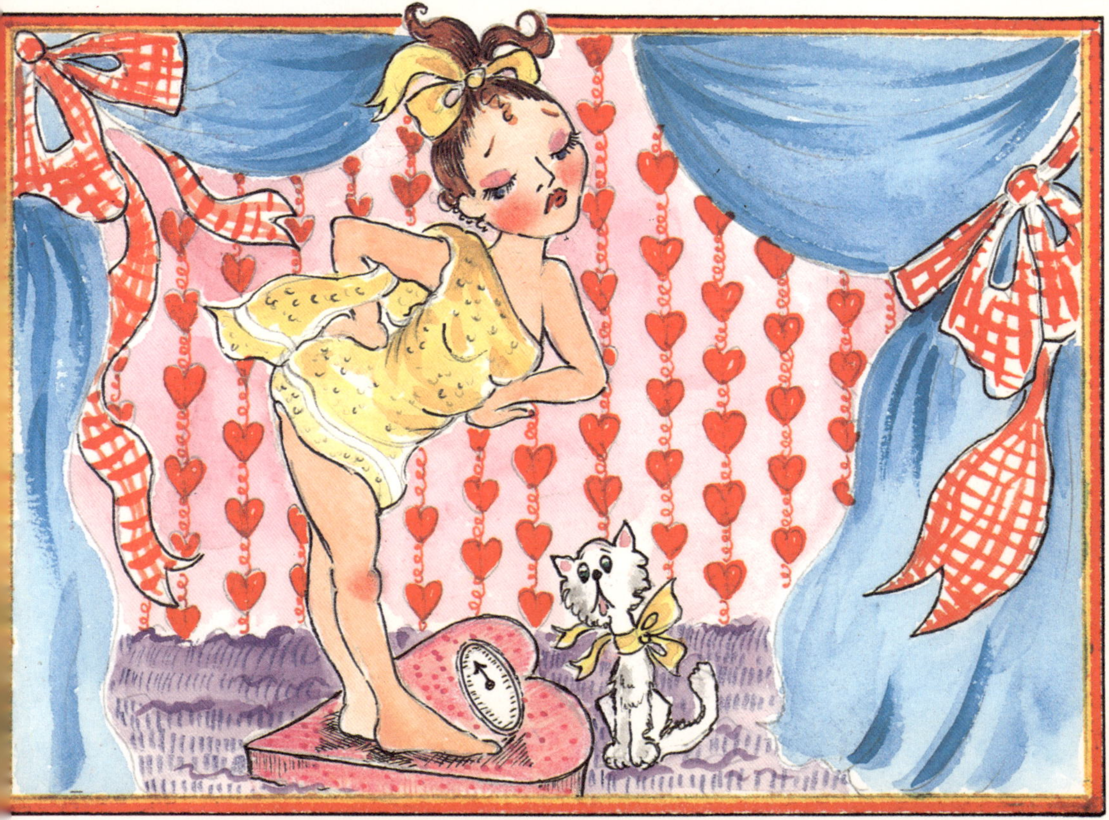

A Friend is Someone Who...

Has seen you through love lost
and weight gained.

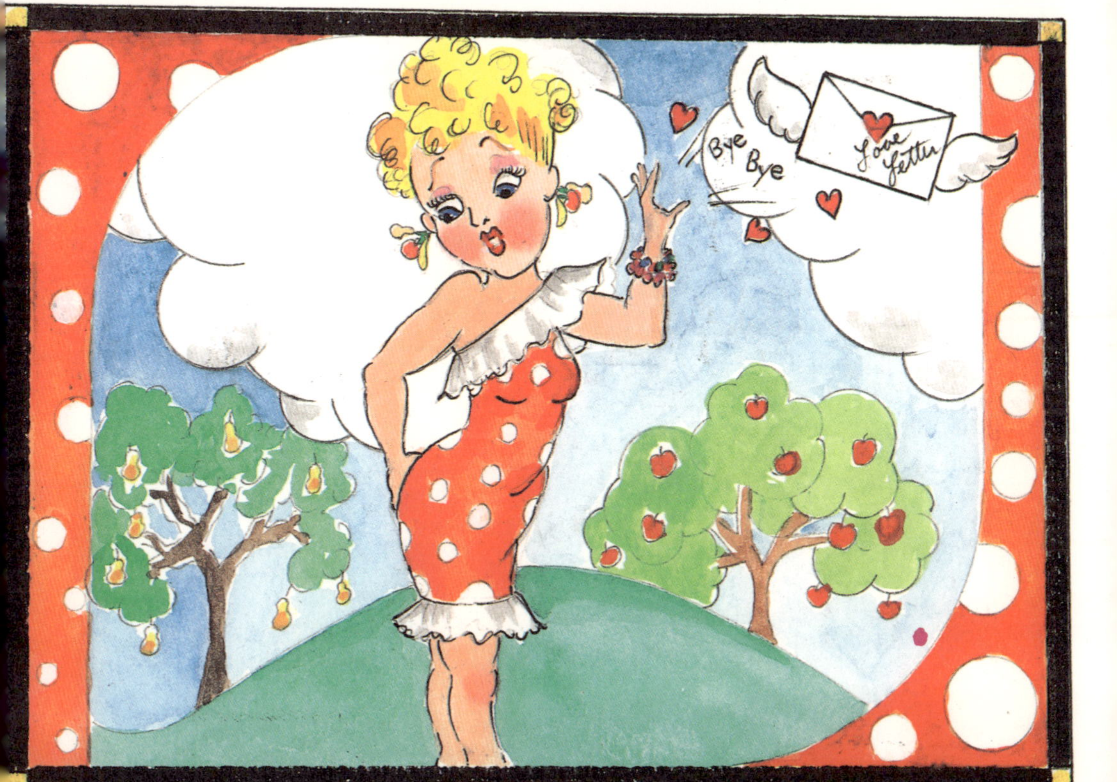
Bye Bye
Love Letter

A Friend is Someone Who...

You can talk to even without words.

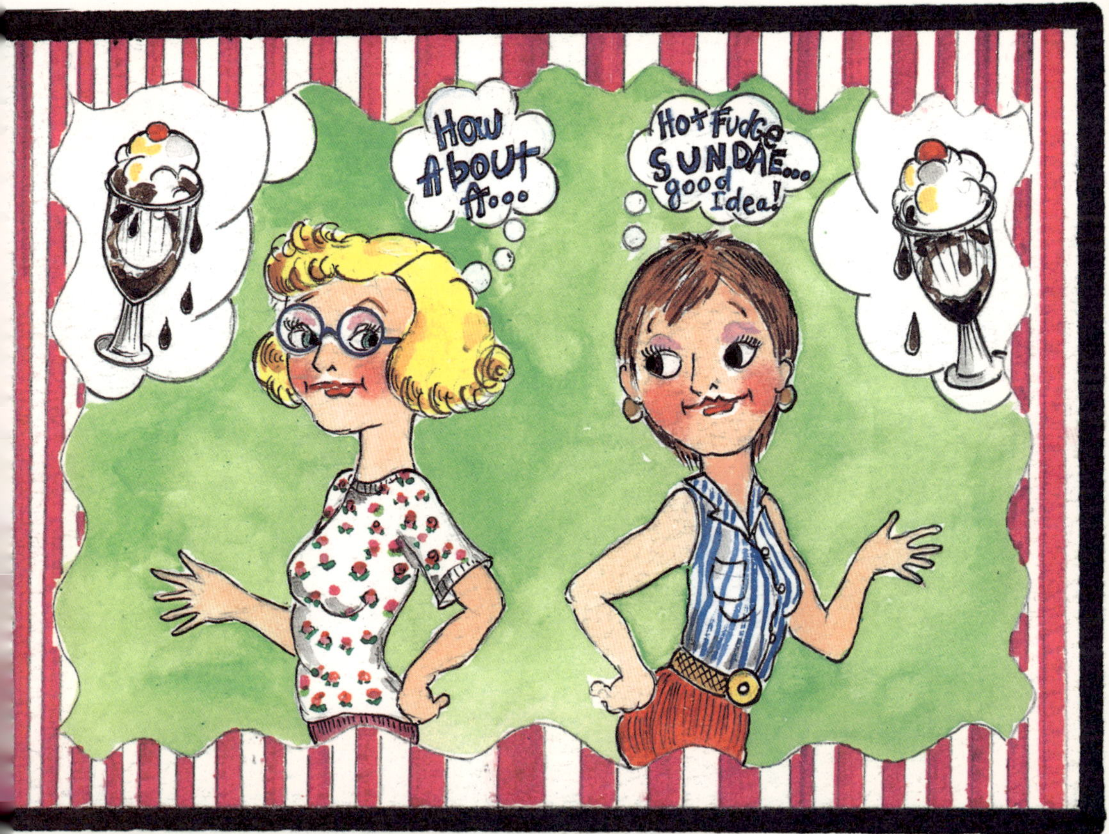
How About A...
Hot Fudge SUNDAE... good Idea!

A Friend is Someone Who...

You can share your
New Year's resolutions with.

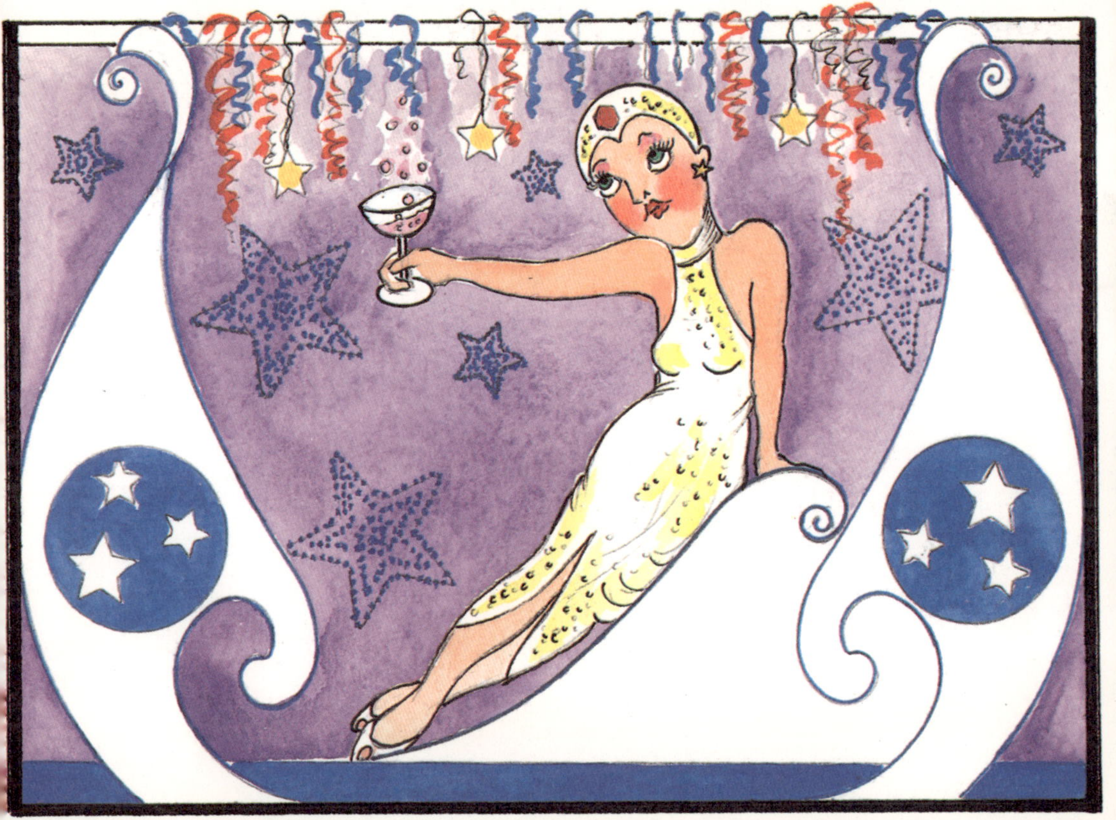

A Friend is Someone Who...

Makes you feel whole when you're

coming apart.

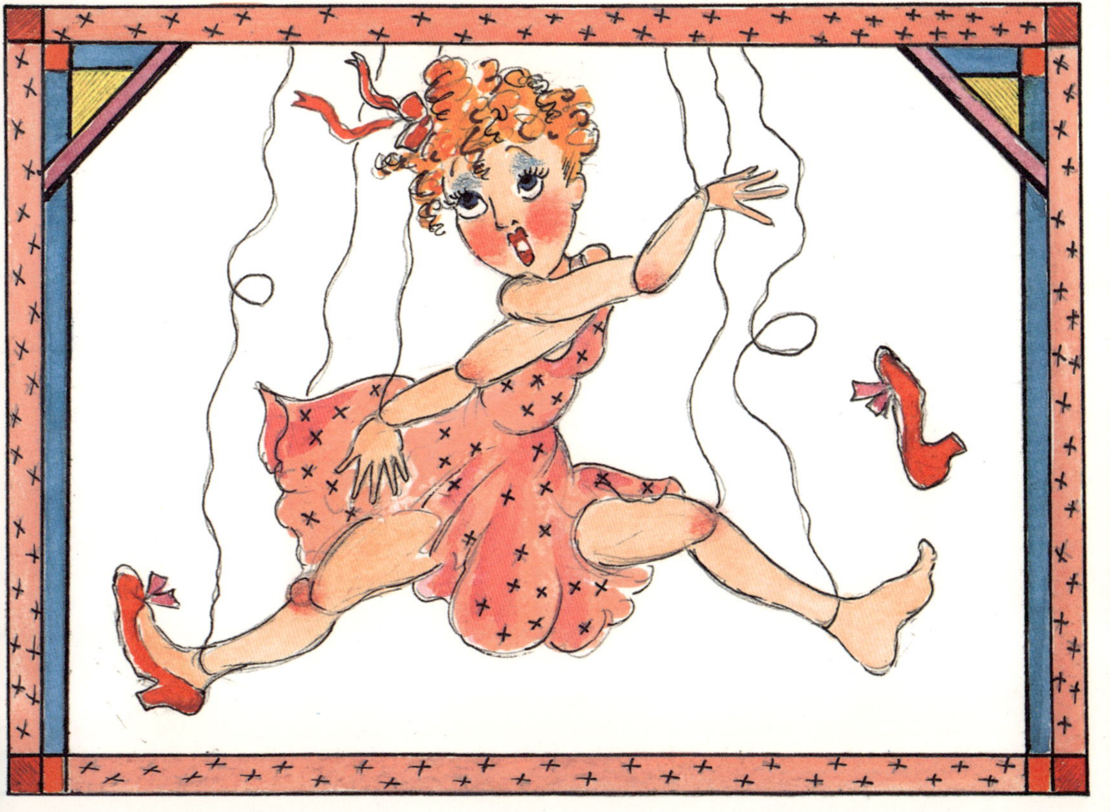

A Friend is Someone Who...

Keeps your deep, dark secrets
under lock and key.

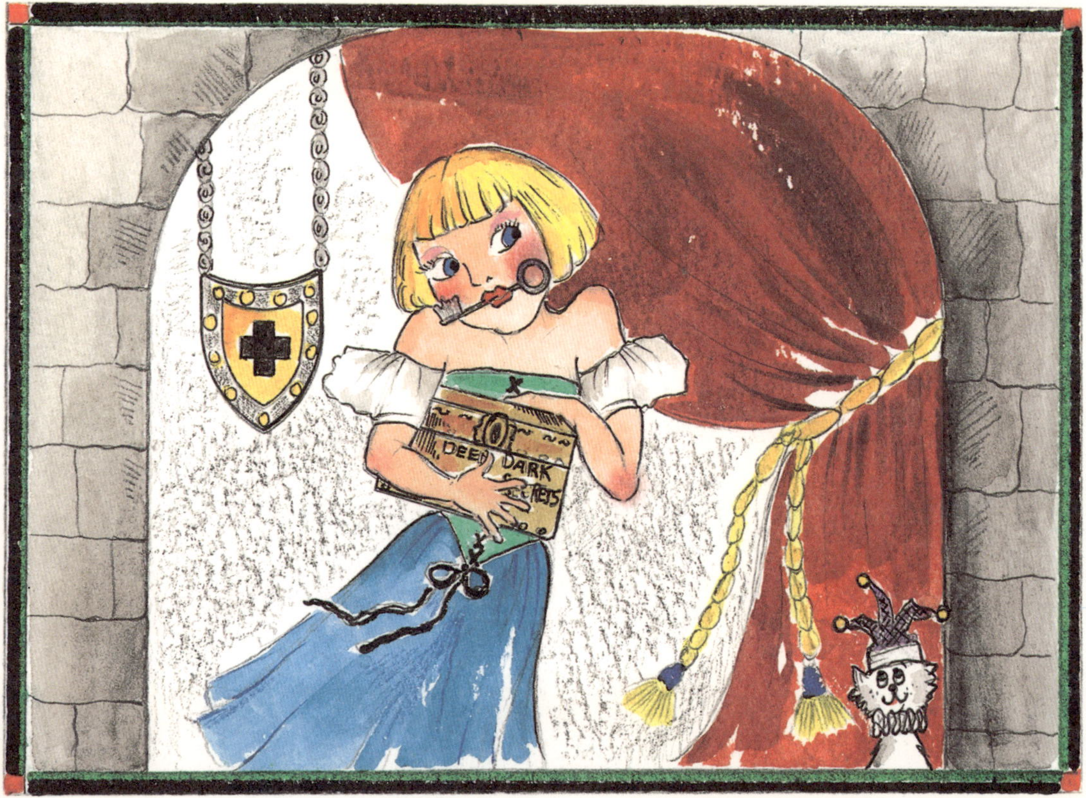
DARK

A Friend is Someone Who...

Reminds you of all that is good in people.

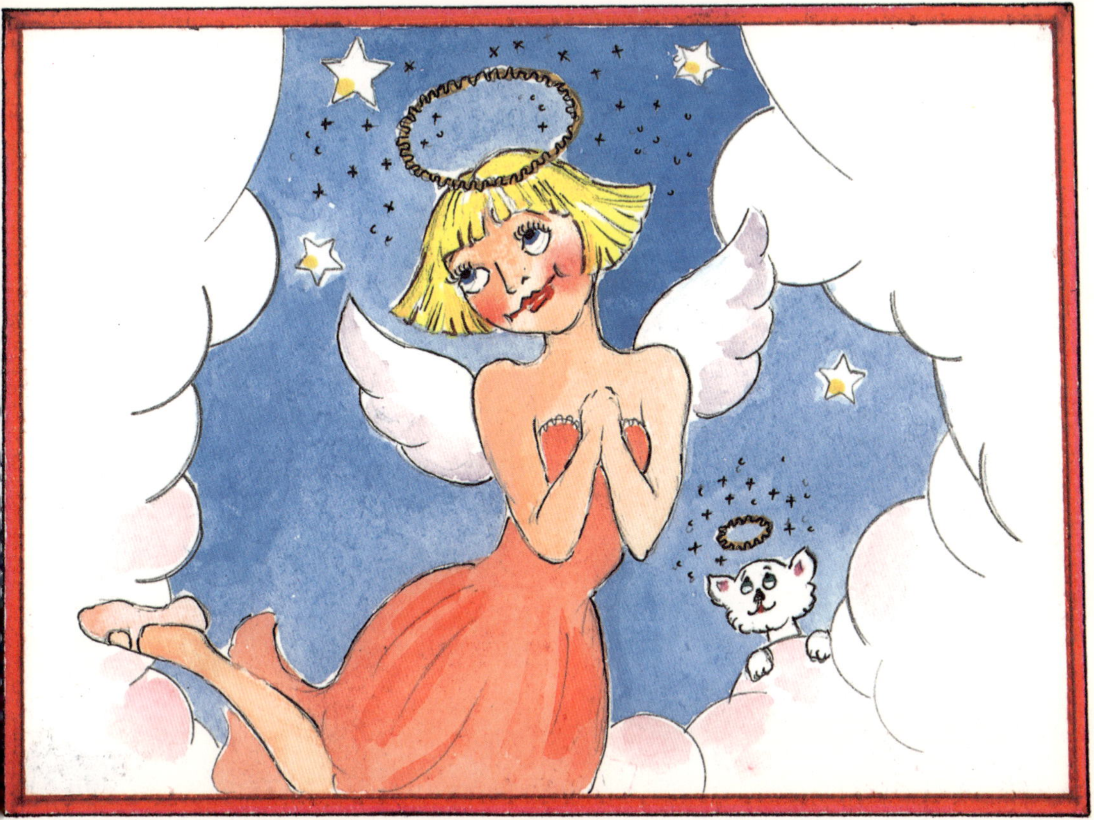

A Friend is Someone Who...

Can make a supermarket outing
feel like an adventure.

TATOES
LB. BAG
LETTUCE
99¢
CARROTS
50¢ BUNCH
WATER
GOODY
CRACKERS
COOKIES
COOKIES
COOKIES
COOKIES
COOKIES
DUSTER
SALE

A Friend is Someone Who...

Tells you white lies about how good you look on your blue days.

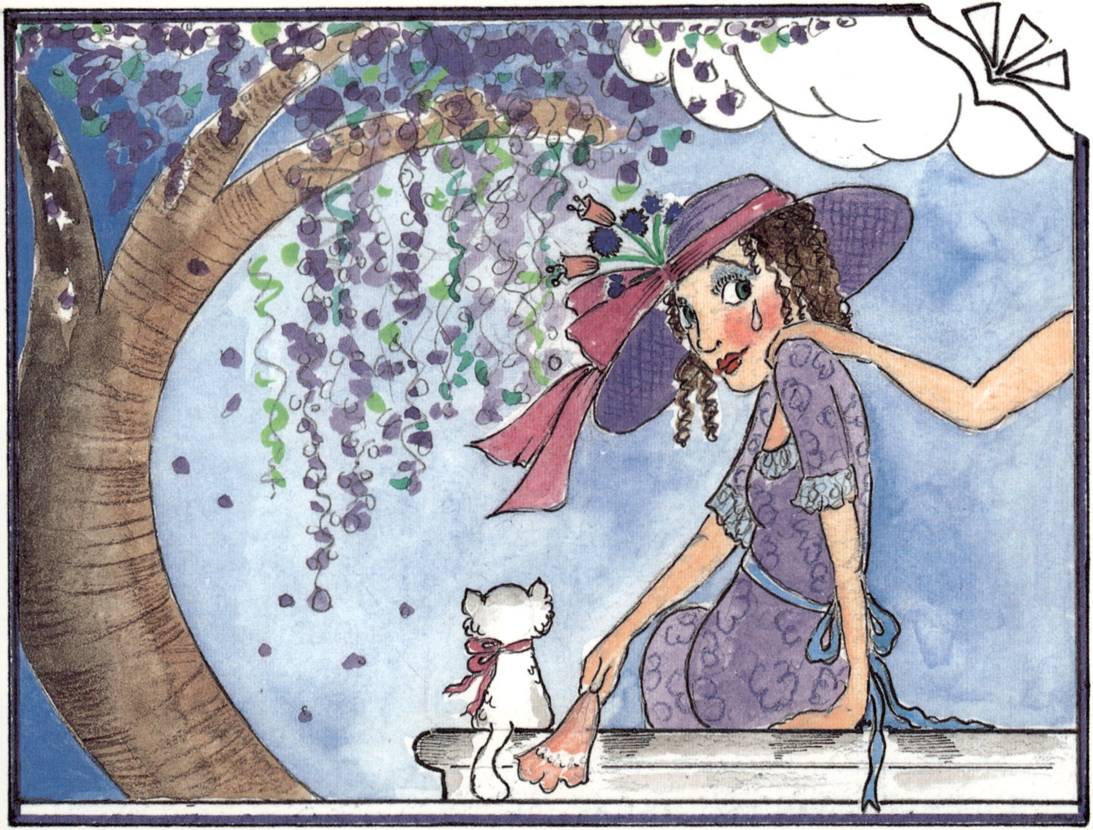

A Friend is Someone Who...

Makes you laugh despite yourself.

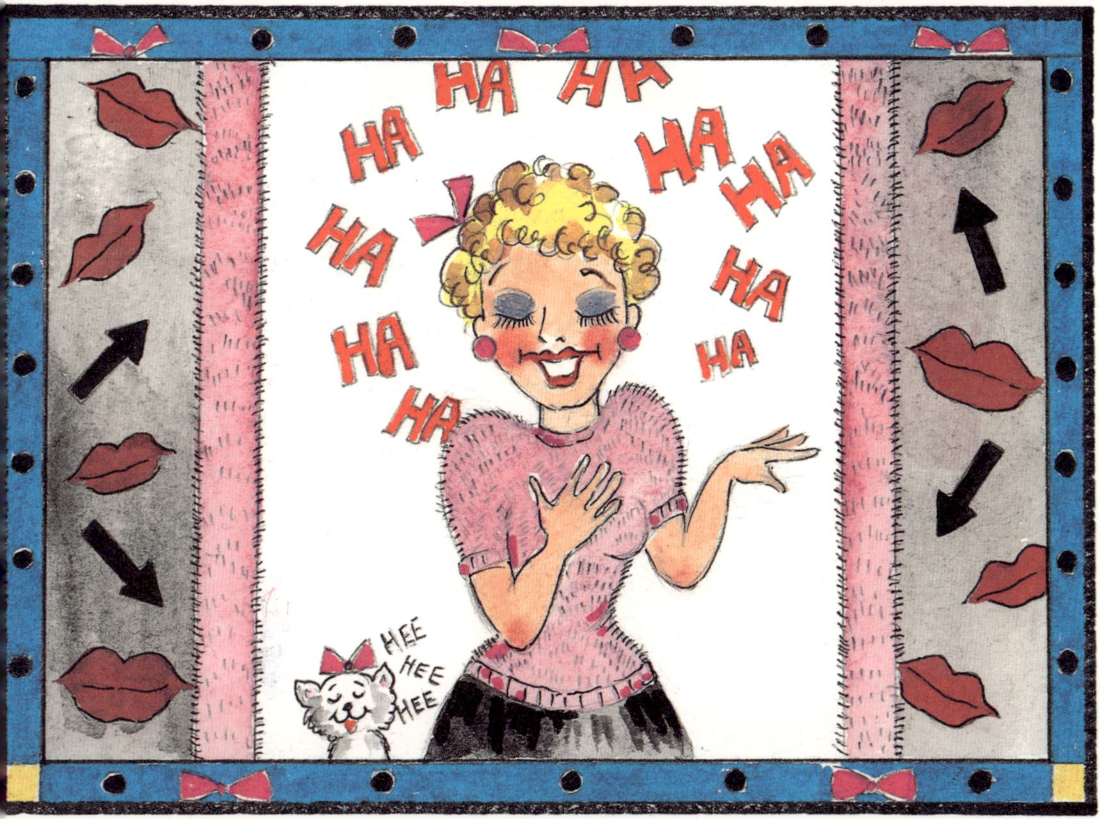
HA HA
HA
HA
HA
HA
HA
HA
HA
HA
HEE
HEE
HEE

A Friend is Someone Who...

Understands you sometimes
need to be alone.

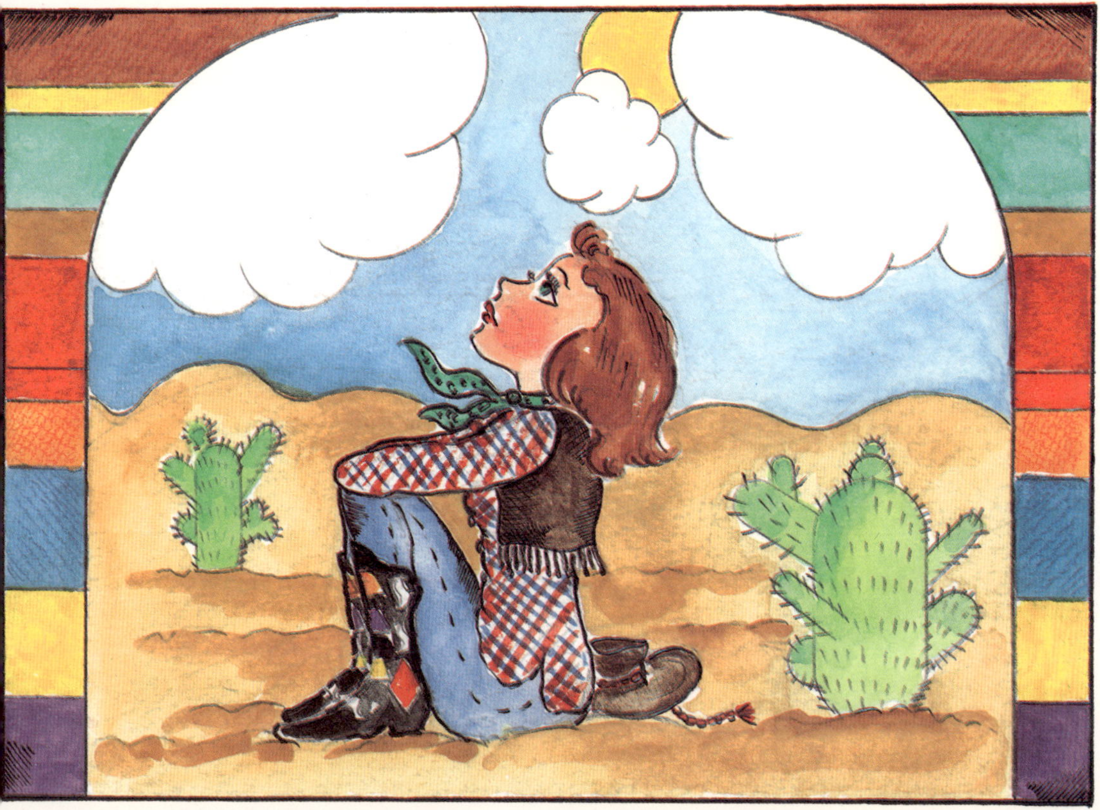

A Friend is Someone Who...

Provides shelter from a storm.

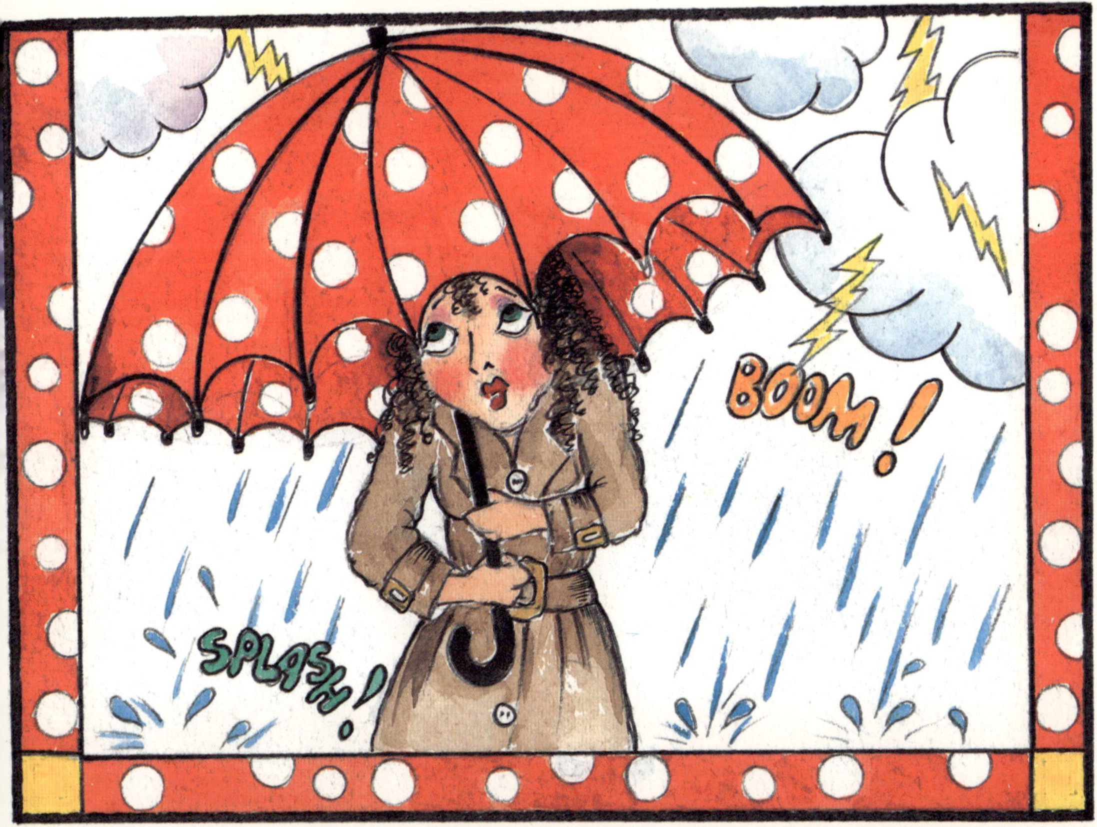
BOOM!
SPLASH!

A Friend is Someone Who...

Defends you when you get into fights
with yourself.

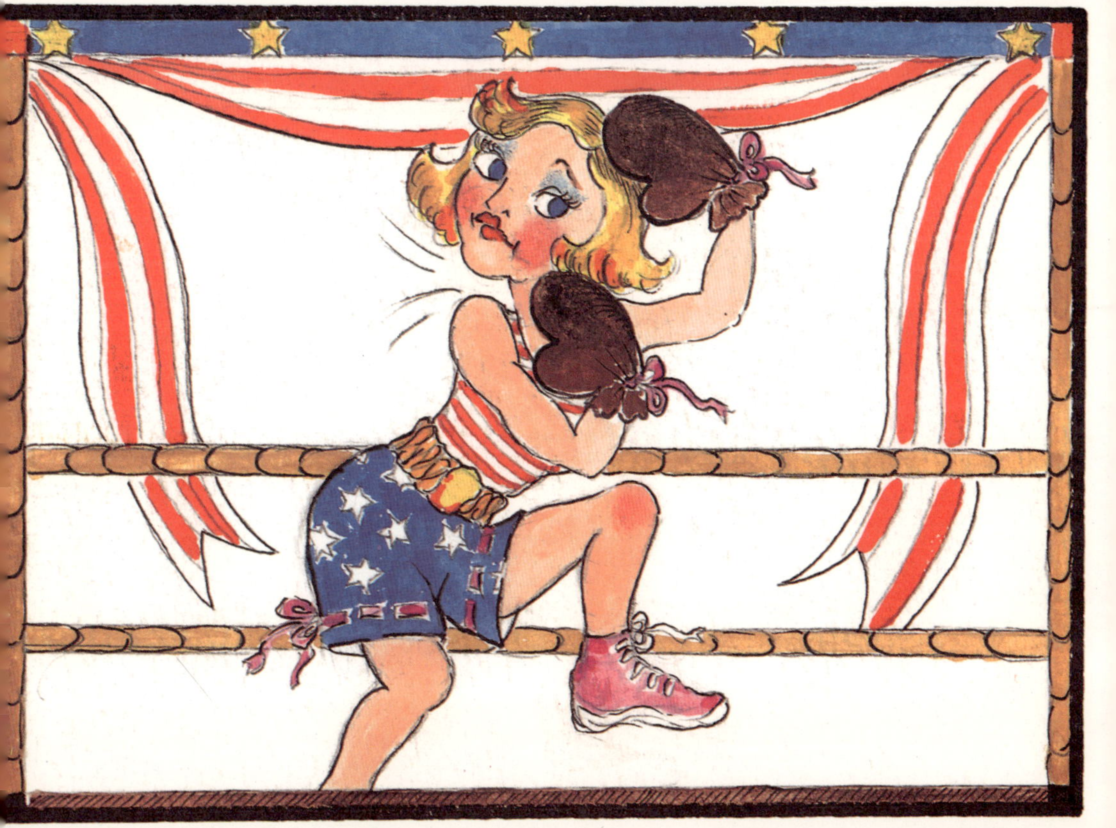

A Friend is Someone Who...

Is your second self.

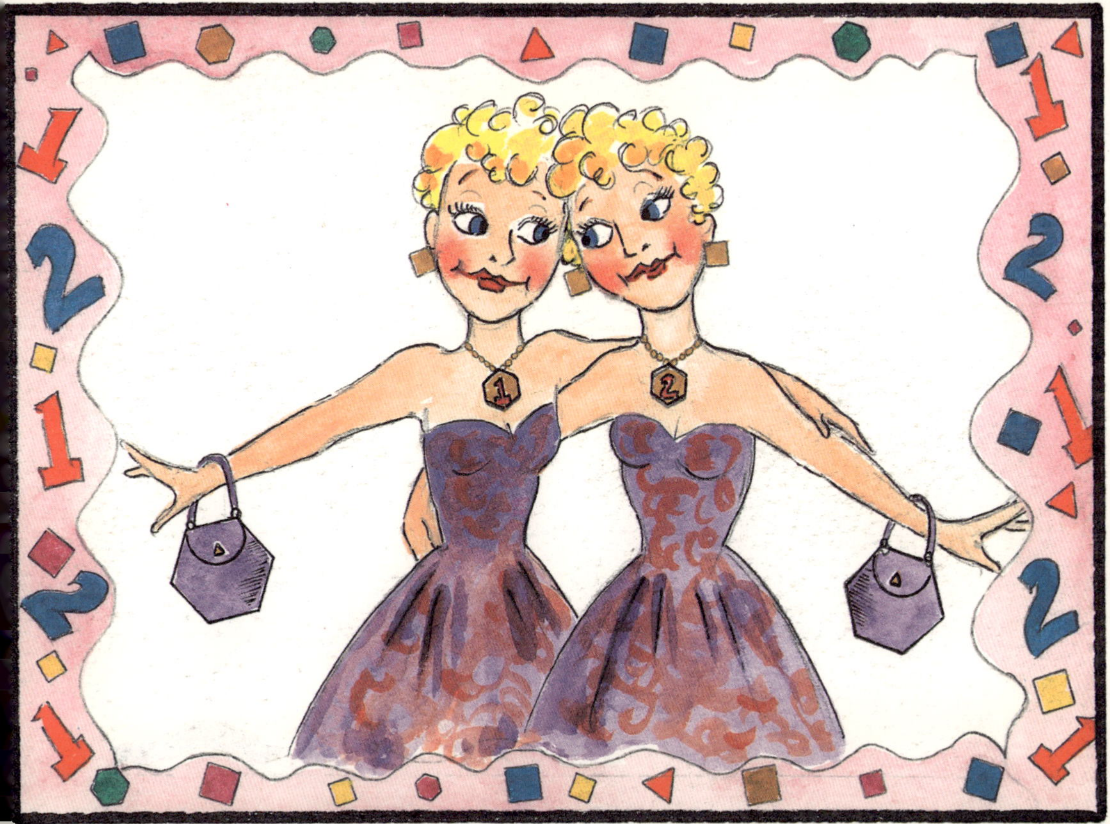

A Friend is Someone Who...

You can be silent with.

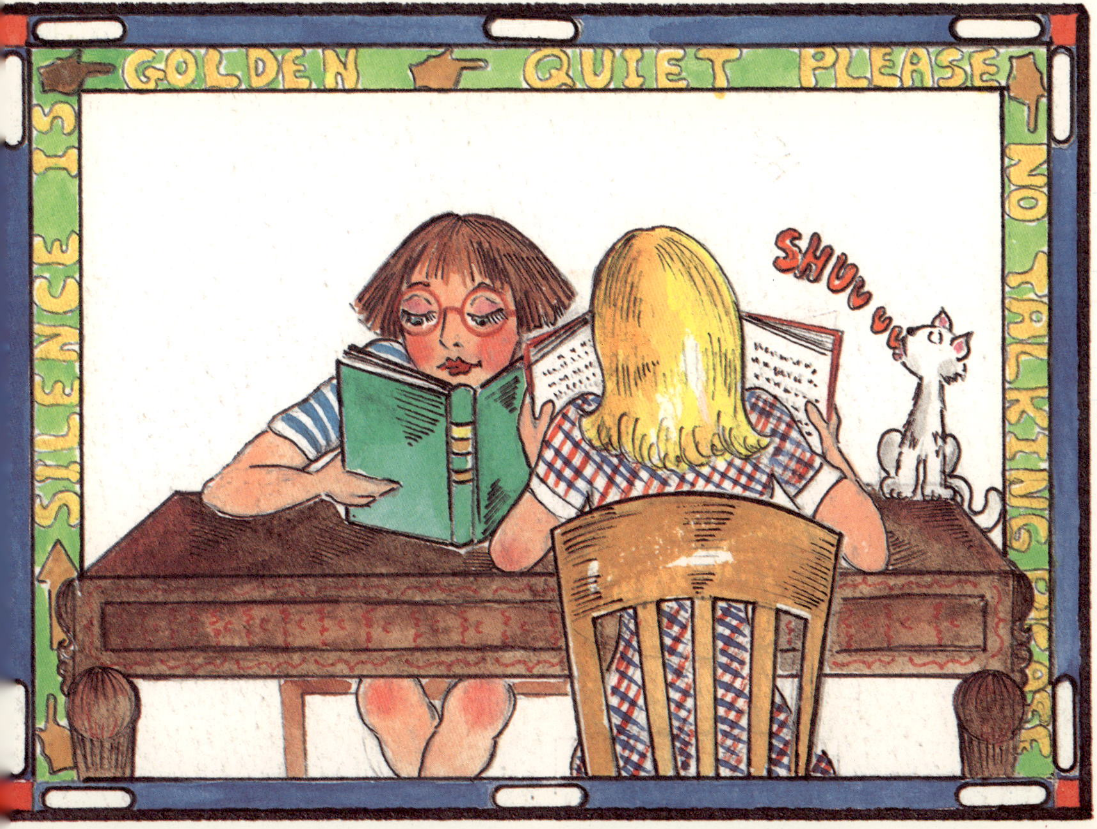
SILENCE IS GOLDEN
QUIET PLEASE
NO TALKING
SHUUUU

A Friend is Someone Who...

Writes letters you want to save.

Feb 28
Dear Debbie:
We really miss
all of you and I can't
LITTLE LETTER BOX

A Friend is Someone Who...

Gives your world a special glow.

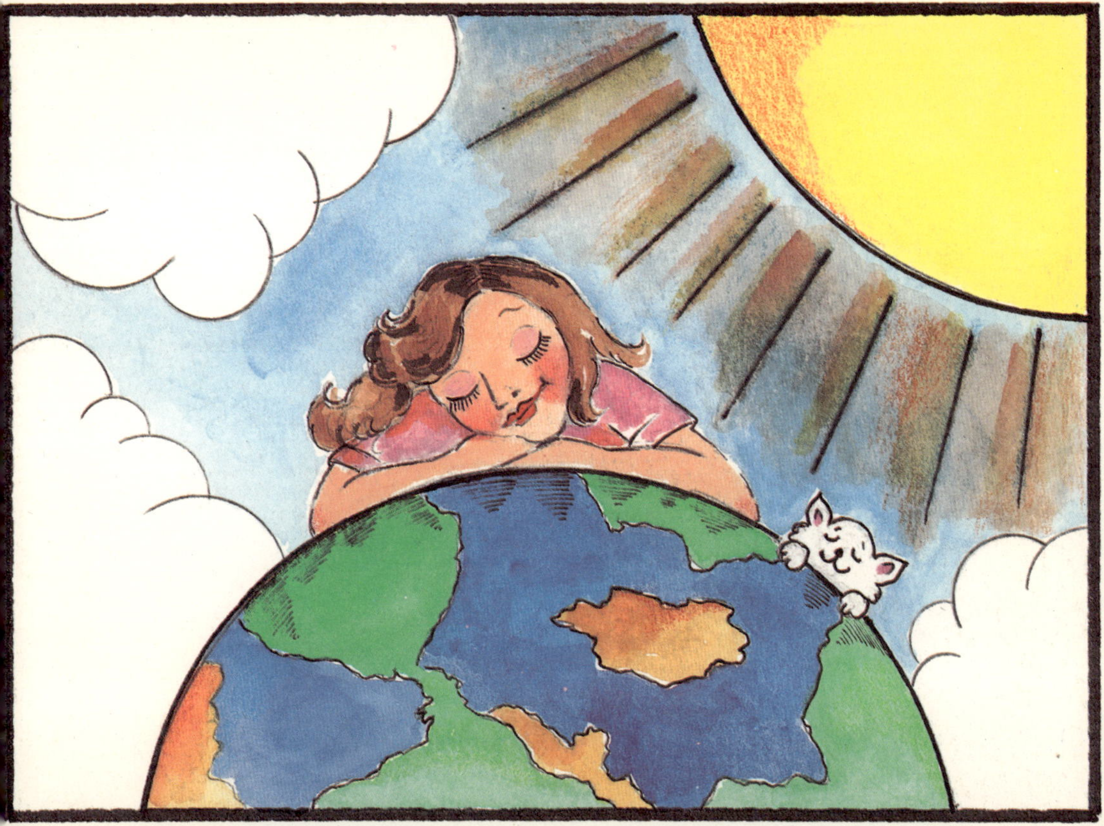